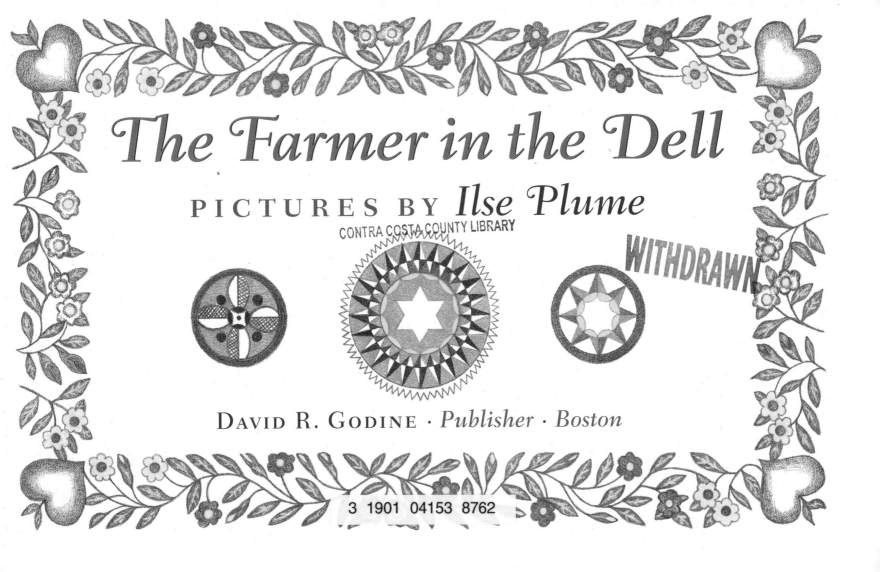

The Farmer in the Dell

PICTURES BY Ilse Plume

DAVID R. GODINE · *Publisher* · *Boston*

First published in 2004 by
David R. Godine, Publisher
Post Office Box 450
Jaffrey, New Hampshire 03452
www.godine.com

Illustrations copyright © 2004 by Ilse Plume

LIBRARY OF CONGRESS CATALOGING-IN-PUBLICATION DATA
The farmer in the dell / illustrated by Ilse Plume.—1st ed.
p.   cm.
Summary: Provides the words to nine verses of the well-known folk song,
with instructions for playing the traditional game.
ISBN 1–56792–270–8 (alk. paper)
1. Folk songs, English–United States—Texts. 2. Children's songs, English—United States—Texts.
[1. Farm life—Songs and music. 2. Folk songs—United States. 3. Singing games.]
I. Plume, Ilse, ill. II. Title
PZ8.3.F2285   2004
782.42162'13'00268—dc22   2004005680

FIRST EDITION
Printed in the United States of America

For my mother Alice
& my daughter
Anne-Marie

The farmer in the dell, the farmer in the dell,

Heigh-ho the derry-o, the farmer in the dell.

The farmer takes a wife, the farmer takes a wife,

Heigh-ho the derry-o, the farmer takes a wife.

The wife takes a child, the wife takes a child,

The child takes a nurse, the child takes a nurse,

Heigh-ho the derry-o, the child takes a nurse.

The nurse takes a dog, the nurse takes a dog,

Heigh-ho the derry-o, the nurse takes a dog.

The dog takes a cat, the dog takes a cat,

Heigh-ho the derry-o, the dog takes a cat.

The cat takes a rat, the cat takes a rat,

Heigh-ho the derry-o, the cat takes a rat.

The rat takes the cheese, the rat takes the cheese,

Heigh-ho the derry-o, the rat takes the cheese.

The cheese stands alone, the cheese stands alone,

Heigh-ho the derry-o, the cheese stands alone.

How to Play *The Farmer in the Dell*

THE FARMER IN THE DELL begins with a group of children forming a circle around a single child who is designated "the farmer." As the children begin to sing the song, they hold hands and dance in a circle around the farmer. When the children sing "The farmer takes a wife, the farmer takes a wife, heigh-ho the derry-o, the farmer takes a wife," the child in the center of the circle chooses another child to come into the center with him, and she is designated "the wife."

The farmer can select his wife either by spinning around with his eyes closed and choosing the child to whom he randomly points, or he can actively choose a specific child. The game continues in the same manner with the wife picking a "child," then the child picking a "nurse," and so on until the seventh child becomes "the rat."

When all of the children in the circle sing "The rat takes the cheese, the rat takes the cheese, heigh-ho the derry-o, the rat takes the cheese," the eighth child is chosen and as she enters the circle the other players go back into the circle, join hands with the other children, and sing along: "The cheese stands alone, the cheese stands alone, heigh-ho the derry-o, the cheese stands alone."

To begin the next round of the game, the cheese is designated the farmer and she chooses the next wife.

The farmer in the dell, the farmer in the dell,
   Heigh-ho the derry-o, the farmer in the dell.
The farmer takes a wife, the farmer takes a wife,
   Heigh-ho the derry-o, the farmer takes a wife.
The wife takes a child, the wife takes a child,
   Heigh-ho the derry-o, the wife takes a child.
The child takes a nurse, the child takes a nurse,
   Heigh-ho the derry-o, the child takes a nurse.
The nurse takes a dog, the nurse takes a dog,
   Heigh-ho the derry-o, the nurse takes a dog.
The dog takes a cat, the dog takes a cat,
   Heigh-ho the derry-o, the dog takes a cat.
The cat takes a rat, the cat takes a rat,
   Heigh-ho the derry-o, the cat takes a rat.
The rat takes the cheese, the rat takes the cheese,
   Heigh-ho the derry-o, the rat takes the cheese.
The cheese stands alone, the cheese stands alone,
   Heigh-ho the derry-o, the cheese stands alone.

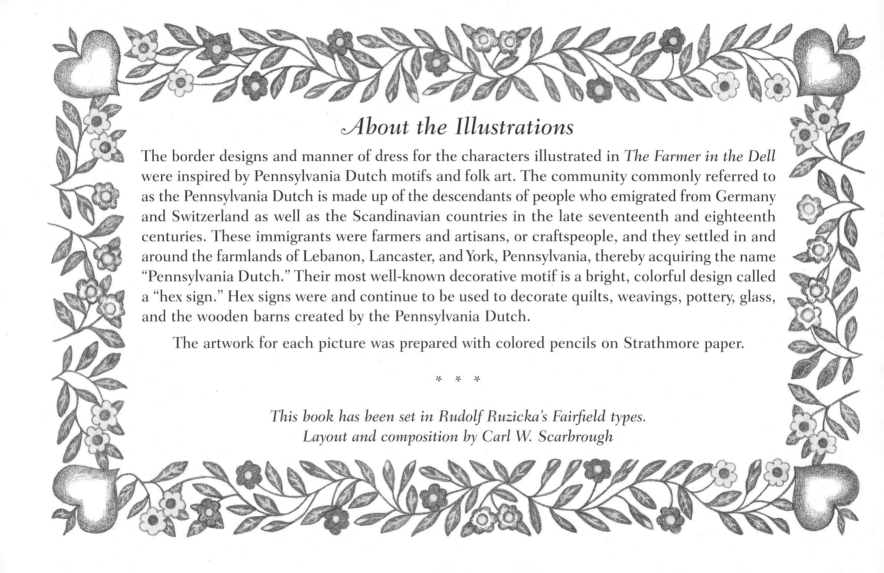

About the Illustrations

The border designs and manner of dress for the characters illustrated in *The Farmer in the Dell* were inspired by Pennsylvania Dutch motifs and folk art. The community commonly referred to as the Pennsylvania Dutch is made up of the descendants of people who emigrated from Germany and Switzerland as well as the Scandinavian countries in the late seventeenth and eighteenth centuries. These immigrants were farmers and artisans, or craftspeople, and they settled in and around the farmlands of Lebanon, Lancaster, and York, Pennsylvania, thereby acquiring the name "Pennsylvania Dutch." Their most well-known decorative motif is a bright, colorful design called a "hex sign." Hex signs were and continue to be used to decorate quilts, weavings, pottery, glass, and the wooden barns created by the Pennsylvania Dutch.

The artwork for each picture was prepared with colored pencils on Strathmore paper.

* * *

This book has been set in Rudolf Ruzicka's Fairfield types.
Layout and composition by Carl W. Scarbrough

About the Artist

Born in Dresden, Germany, ILSE PLUME has studied in Florence, Italy, as well as in the United States. She has illustrated many books for children, including The Bremen Town Musicians (a Caldecott Honor Book), The Story of Befana, and The Velveteen Rabbit.

Of Latvian and Lithuanian descent, Plume says, "I could easily relate to the simplicity of Pennsylvania Dutch life. In a way it paralleled my early years as a child of immigrant parents who clung to the heritage and traditions of their homeland.... I recall being dressed in simple clothes of muted colors with the only decorations being the ribbons my grandmother tied in my long braids!"

Soon after their arrival in the U.S., her family settled in Pennsylvania. Later, as a student at the University of Iowa, I lived in "Grant Wood Country" and near the Amana Colonies (an Amish settlement near Iowa City.) I found the colors and the beautiful decorative elements of the Pennsylvania Dutch artists especially intriguing and decided to do some research, which eventually led to the creation of this book.

Ms. Plume created the illustrations for this book in her sunny studio at the Emerson Umbrella, in Concord, Massachusetts. When not making picture books, she teaches illustration at the School of the Museum of Fine Arts, Boston.